To Grampy

Merry Christmas

Yea, It's Hokie Game Day!

Cheryl and Frank Beamer

Illustrated by Miguel De Angel

www.mascotbooks.com

It was game day in Blacksburg, Virginia.
Two little Hokies were headed to
Lane Stadium with their family.

They stopped at the Hokie Bird
statue on Main Street. The little Hokies
said, "Yea, it's Hokie game day!"

The little Hokies headed to the
bookstore where they found lots of
Virginia Tech stuff.

"Yea, it's Hokie game day!"
cheered the bookstore worker.

The little Hokies arrived at Lane Stadium.
Hamburgers, hotdogs, and turkey legs
were cooking on the grill.

Children were playing football and
getting their faces painted.
"Yea, it's Hokie game day!" they cheered.

The little Hokies spotted
Hokie Bird outside Lane Stadium.
"Hello, Hokie Bird!" said the children.

Hokie Bird posed for pictures with fans.
"Yea, it's Hokie game day!"
said the fans.

The little Hokies went to the "The Walk."
Thousands of Hokies lined the street
to welcome the team.

Coach Beamer led the football team
as the crowd cheered,
"Yea, it's Hokie game day!"

The little Hokies entered Lane Stadium.
Meanwhile, Coach Beamer encouraged
the team to play their best.

"Yea, it's Hokie game day!"
said Coach Beamer.

It was time for the Virginia Tech Hokies to take the field. As they ran out, each player touched the Hokie Stone.

"Yea, it's Hokie game day,"
cheered the players.

Virginia Tech scored a touchdown!
The cannon was fired and Hokie Bird
lifted weights for every point scored.

"One, two, three, four, five, six, seven,"
counted the fans. "Yea, it's Hokie game
day!" said the cheerleaders.

At halftime the Marching Virginians
performed "Tech Triumph," the
"Old Hokie" cheer, and the "Hokie Pokey."

"Hokie, Hokie, Hokie, Hi!"
cheered the little Hokies.

The Virginia Tech Hokies
won the football game!
The crowd cheered for the team.

The little Hokies gave each other
a high-five. They said,
"Yea, it's a Hokie victory day!"

After the game, the little Hokies
waited for autographs from
their favorite Virginia Tech players.

Hokie game day was over.
The little Hokies had a fun and tiring day.
"Good night, little Hokies."

This book is dedicated to the memory of two special people.

The first is my daddy, Mike Oakley. And, yes, I still call him "daddy" – it's a Southern thing…

He was not perfect but he was always striving to be so in mine and my sister's eyes by the way he lived his life.

They say little girls marry someone like their father. Well, I did just that! Daddy was honest, fair, unselfish, hardworking and did nothing to bring praise to himself (though he deserved it on many occasion). He gave quietly. Frank is the same way; he just has a public stage and arena. Shane and Casey did not have enough time with Daddy as he died in 1989, but they were around him long enough to learn some of the same things I did and to form some memories of their own.

He probably would have liked to have had a son but ended up with two girls. He did get two great sons through the marriage of those two girls. He also had two grandsons – and two granddaughters. Two great granddaughters and a great grandson was added to the mix but he never had the pleasure of knowing him.

What I, and all of us in our family, would have cherished would have been to have him much longer. What joy he would have had sharing who he was with what we became because of his influence and love.

The other special person is my brother-in-law, Waddey Harvey. He was a great Hokie football player. He and Frank played football together at Tech and Waddey actually hand picked Frank to take me out.

Waddey was a great daddy, too. His son Jay is a Tech graduate (as is his wife Lisa) and it is Jay's children, Kendyl and Jake, who are the likeness of the two Hokie children in this book. Kendyl actually gave me insight as to what kids like about game day.

Waddey would have been pleased to see that Jay has instilled in them what being a Hokie is all about.

Hope all of you can relate to game day as seen through the eyes of a child. After all, we are all Hokie kids at heart.

Enjoy!

Cheryl

Cheryl Beamer

I would like to take this opportunity to say thanks to the most caring person ever - my wife, Cheryl. She has been a great coach's wife, during the good times and the bad, and has been steady in both. She has been the greatest Mom for Shane and Casey (if it was possible, it was going to happen for them). She has been a terrific friend for 34 years.

Frank

Frank Beamer

For Sue, Ana Milagros, and Angel Miguel ~ Miguel De Angel

For more information about our products, please visit us online at www.mascotbooks.com.

For more information, please contact Mascot Books,
P.O. Box 220157, Chantilly, VA 20153-0157

ISBN: 1-932888-44-6

Printed in the United States.

www.mascotbooks.com